C8 000 000 434287

PUFFIN BOOKS

FREAKY FAMILIES

Great-aunt Iris Goes Hunting

Karen Wallace was born in Canada and spent her childhood messing about on the river in the backwoods of Quebec. Now she lives in Herefordshire with her husband – the author Sam Llewellyn – two sons and a cat called Cougar.

DISCARD

Che
or t(
www.
www

50706

Some other books by Karen Wallace

CREAKIE HALL: ACE GHOSTS
CREAKIE HALL: GHOULS RULE
CREAKIE HALL: FUNKY PHANTOMS
CREAKIE HALL: STAR SPOOKS

Karen Wallace

Freaky Families

Great-aunt Iris
Goes Hunting

Illustrated by Colin Paine

PUFFIN BOOKS

PUFFIN BOOKS

Published by the Penguin Group
Penguin Books Ltd, 27 Wrights Lane, London W8 5TZ, England
Penguin Books USA Inc., 375 Hudson Street, New York, New York 10014, USA
Penguin Books Australia Ltd, Ringwood, Victoria, Australia
Penguin Books Canada Ltd, 10 Alcorn Avenue, Toronto, Ontario, Canada M4V 3B2
Penguin Books (NZ) Ltd, 182–190 Wairau Road, Auckland 10, New Zealand

Penguin Books Ltd, Registered Offices: Harmondsworth, Middlesex, England

First published 1998
3 5 7 9 10 8 6 4 2

Text copyright © Karen Wallace, 1998
Illustrations copyright © Colin Paine, 1998
All rights reserved

The moral right of the author and illustrator has been asserted

Except in the United States of America, this book is sold subject to the condition that
it shall not, by way of trade or otherwise, be lent, re-sold, hired out, or otherwise
circulated without the publisher's prior consent in any form of binding or cover
other than that in which it is published and without a similar condition including
this condition being imposed on the subsequent purchaser

Filmset in Times New Roman

Printed in Hong Kong by Midas Printing Ltd

British Library Cataloguing in Publication Data
A CIP catalogue record for this book is available from the British Library

ISBN 0–140–38499–5

··· Contents ···

1. Gardens and Good Manners

Mr and Mrs Primly-Proper lived in a neat house on a tidy street with their two children, Jack and Daisy.

Every Saturday morning, Mr Primly-Proper washed the car.

Mrs Primly-Proper clipped the
hedge. Jack mowed the lawn and
Daisy polished the two gnomes on
toadstools in the garden.

It was the same every week,
every year.

One Saturday morning, after
breakfast, a letter arrived.

"Great-aunt Iris Myrtleberrie

has asked Jack and Daisy to stay,"
said Mr Primly-Proper as he read
the letter.

Jack and Daisy looked at each
other and sighed. Great-aunt Iris
was a keen gardener. All she ever
talked about was gardening. She
even held up her long white hair
with a tiny gold gardening fork.

There was only one thing that Jack and Daisy knew about gardening – it was boring.

"What a lovely idea," chirped Mrs Primly-Proper, untying her frilly apron and folding it neatly over the back of her chair. "When do we need to leave?"

Mr Primly-Proper stood up. "This afternoon," he said. "After I've washed the car."

Great-aunt Iris Myrtleberrie lived in a pink and white cottage in the middle of a maze. When she invited people to stay (which wasn't often because she was always busy gardening), she left a trail of pink and white shells to show the way.

The maze was thick and made of huge bushes covered in shiny leaves.

"There are only two things Great-aunt Iris *really* cares about," said Mr Primly-Proper as they followed the path of shells to the pink and white cottage. "Gardens and good manners."

"And there are only two things she gets *really* angry about," added Mrs Primly-Proper. "Weeds and bad manners."

2. Can You Keep a Secret?

After their parents had left, Jack and Daisy sat at the tea table with their Great-aunt Iris. They were trying so hard to be polite that neither of them had yet spoken.

"Where do all your plants come from?" asked Daisy, at last.

"From all over the world," replied Great-aunt Iris, sipping tea from a tiny cup. "Plants grow in the strangest places."

"I thought all plants came from seed packets," said Jack, whose finger was stuck in the teacup's tiny handle.

As Great-aunt Iris laughed and shook her head, the telephone rang. She picked it up, frowned and rushed from the room.

"What are we going to *do*?" whispered Jack, tugging desperately at his teacup. "We're stuck here for a week."

Daisy had thought the same thing. What was there to do? Prune roses? Pick caterpillars off cabbages?

Weed carrots? "Go crazy," she said.

Then Great-aunt Iris rushed back into the room and Jack and Daisy thought their eyes would pop out!

Great-aunt Iris was dressed in commando gear and her white hair hung in two long braids halfway down her back!

"Can you keep a secret?" asked Great-aunt Iris. Her voice was low and urgent.

"Y-y-yes," stammered Jack and Daisy. They were so astonished they could barely speak.

"I'm not only a gardener," said Great-aunt Iris. As she spoke, she pulled a knife out of a drawer and stuffed it through her belt.

"I'm a *plant-hunter*. And you're coming with me on an important mission."

"We are?" gasped Jack and Daisy.

"You are!" replied Great-aunt Iris. She pulled the tail of a china dog that sat on the sideboard.

A trapdoor slid open in the middle of the room.

Jack stared at Daisy. They were both thinking the same thing. If their parents knew for one minute that –

"Follow me!" cried Great-aunt Iris.

Without a second thought, Jack and Daisy ran down a flight of steps and along a tunnel. When they came out the other end, they were standing on a private airfield, hidden in another part of the maze.

A jet was ready and waiting.
"Grey-Matter Motors" was written
along the side.

"Where are we going?" asked
Daisy as they flew high over the
pink and white cottage.

"To a secret laboratory in the
middle of a jungle in South

America," said Great-aunt Iris.
"A shrinking violet has been
discovered."

"I thought a shrinking violet was
someone who was shy at parties,"
said Jack.

"That's one kind of shrinking
violet," said Great-aunt Iris.

Her blue eyes sparkled like fireworks. "But this shrinking violet actually *shrinks* people."

Jack gasped. "You mean –"

Great-aunt Iris held up her hand. "No more questions now," she said firmly. Then she leaned back in her seat, pulled a black mask over her eyes and went to sleep.

Daisy looked sideways at Jack. "Who said gardening was boring?" she whispered with a big grin on her face.

3. No Time to Lose!

In a secret laboratory in the middle of a jungle in South America, a scientist called Dr Grey-Matter was waiting.

"Greetings, Miss Myrtleberrie," he cried when Great-aunt Iris walked into the room. "You are just in time."

He pointed to the first of three drawings on a blackboard behind him.

"Look at this man. You will notice he is much bigger than this

matchbox beside him," said Dr Grey-Matter.

He pointed to the second drawing. "Here is the shrinking violet. You will see the man is eating the shrinking violet."

He pointed to the third drawing.

"Here is the man again. You will see he is the same size as the matchbox."

His eyes blazed. "Spot the difference, Miss Myrtleberrie!" he cried.

Great-aunt Iris went white. "If this shrinking violet gets into the wrong hands . . ." she said slowly.

"Anything could happen!" shouted Jack.

"The future of the world is at stake!" cried Daisy.

"Clever children!" beamed Dr Grey-Matter. He pointed through the window to a volcano sticking up out of the jungle. "The shrinking violet grows there. But I don't know exactly where."

"We'll find it!" cried Great-aunt Iris. "Come along, dears! There's no time to lose!"

4. Anything for a Dollar

That night, Great-aunt Iris hired a steamboat to take them upriver towards the volcano.

The steamboat was owned by an ugly-looking weasel called Dirty Dollar Dave.

In the middle of the night,

Great-aunt Iris woke up. She knew something was wrong.

She crept out of her cabin and saw three men standing around a lamp in the wheelhouse.

They were wearing raincoats and sunglasses and they had extremely big shoulders.

"Spies," muttered Great-aunt Iris to herself. She crept closer to the door.

"There are two kids and a little old lady," Dirty Dollar Dave was saying. "What do you want me to do with them?"

"Throw 'em overboard," growled the spies.

"Anything for a dollar," replied Dirty Dollar Dave. "Follow me."

"Disgraceful manners!" muttered Great-aunt Iris. As Dirty Dollar Dave and the three spies stumped on to the deck, she stuck her foot across the wheelhouse door.

They all tripped and one after another they fell into the river.

"That'll teach 'em," said Great-aunt Iris. Then she made herself comfortable in the wheelhouse and steered the steamer with her foot.

5. Dive! Dive! Dive!

The next morning, they came to a clearing.

Three tiny aeroplanes were parked in a row. "Grey-Matter Motors" was painted on their sides.

"This is our stop," said Great-aunt Iris, tying up the boat. "Know anything about flying?"

The only thing Jack and Daisy knew about flying was that Mr and Mrs Primly-Proper thought it was very, very dangerous.

"We'll learn!" they cried.

A few moments later, they were flying over the jungle towards the volcano.

Suddenly, another plane appeared in the sky!

Three men in sunglasses were flying straight towards them!

"Dive! Dive! Dive!" yelled Great-aunt Iris.

Jack and Daisy followed as Great-aunt Iris dropped out of the sky and landed halfway down the side of the volcano.

All around them drums were

beating and hundreds of smiling people were dancing in a huge circle.

"What fun!" cried Great-aunt Iris. "I love a festival!"

She clambered out of the cockpit.

"You never know who you might meet!" she said.

In the middle of the circle, a man wearing a gold and scarlet cloak jumped and twirled. He wore a crown of high feathers and waved a pole carved with a rabbit's head.

"But, Great-aunt Iris!" cried Jack. "What about the shrinking violet?"

"We'll never find it now," wailed Daisy because Jack and Daisy knew what happened when grown-ups got together at a party – it was impossible to drag them away.

Then again, Great-aunt Iris was no ordinary grown-up.

"Don't worry about the shrinking violet," said Great-aunt Iris in a determined voice. "I'll bet the biggest pumpkin in my garden that the man wearing the crown knows where it is."

"But how will you find out?" cried Jack. "He won't understand a word you're saying!"

"Quite right, dear," cried Great-aunt Iris and her eyes glittered. "I'll dance it!"

Jack and Daisy stared in
amazement as Great-aunt Iris

jumped into the middle of the circle. Her long braids flew around her head. She kicked her legs and spun her arms. She danced the most extraordinary dance.

It was called: *Where does the shrinking violet grow?*

The man wearing the crown was delighted. He danced the answer immediately. *Inside the volcano, halfway down on a mossy ledge. I'll take you, if you want.*

Yes, please, danced Great-aunt Iris.

So everyone danced along a narrow path up the volcano. On the way they picked vines and tied them together to make one long rope.

Then, as the sun began to set, they gave the rope to Great-aunt Iris and danced all the way down again.

"What nice young people," said Great-aunt Iris as she yanked the rope to test its strength.

"Phew!" gasped Jack and Daisy. They were tired out after all the dancing.

Great-aunt Iris wasn't even out of breath.

"Get some sleep," she said, handing them blankets from her backpack. "Tomorrow's going to be a busy day."

6. Inside the Volcano!

The next morning, Great-aunt Iris made them all cups of tea with lots of sugar. "This is the plan," she said. "I tie one end of the rope around my waist –"

"And we tie the other end around a rock!" cried Jack.

"Exactly!" replied Great-aunt
Iris, looking pleased. "Have you
done this sort of thing before?"

"Not quite," admitted Daisy.
"But we've seen it in a film."

"Good enough," said Great-aunt

Iris, kindly. "So you know what to do when I jump into the volcano?"

Jack and Daisy looked worried. They knew what had happened in the film. And it wasn't good.

"When I tug twice, you pull me up!" cried Great-aunt Iris.

Jack looked at Daisy but neither said a word. Great-aunt Iris must have seen a different film.

"Wait!" cried Daisy. "What happens when –"

But it was too late. Great-aunt Iris had disappeared!

As she climbed down the rope into the volcano, Great-aunt Iris felt the air become warm and steamy. The perfect conditions for a violet, she thought as she hung in the blackness.

She didn't notice the bats that flitted past her head or the fierce yellow eyes that stared at her from cracks in the rock.

Down, down, down she went. The circle of sky at the top grew smaller and smaller and smaller.

Great-aunt Iris remembered the instructions in the special dance – *halfway down on a mossy ledge*.

I *must* be halfway by now, she thought.

She stretched out her arm in the dark. There was a ledge. It felt damp and mossy!

Great-aunt Iris switched on a tiny pencil-torch that she wore on a chain around her neck.

An enormous spider was staring

straight at her!

A plant with furry green leaves and tiny purple flowers was poking out from under his huge, hairy legs. He was sitting on the shrinking violet!

Even Great-aunt Iris had to admit she had never seen a spider as big as this one.

Nevertheless, no spider was going to upset her plans, no matter how huge or how hairy.

"Shoo!" she said in her fiercest voice.

The spider was terrified. He leapt off the ledge immediately and scuttled down the volcano.

Quick as a flash, Great-aunt Iris whipped out her trowel.

She dug up the shrinking violet
and put it in her inside jacket
pocket.

Then she tugged twice on the
rope.

7. Spies!

At the top of the volcano, Jack and Daisy had almost given up hope. In the film they had watched, the rope had gone slack because the heroine had been eaten by a huge spider.

What's more, they had just seen

three men wearing raincoats and sunglasses, climbing up the volcano towards them!

When they felt the tugs, they pulled up the rope as fast as they could.

"Seen anything suspicious?" asked Great-aunt Iris as she untied the rope around her waist.

"Three men!" cried Jack.

"With awfully big shoulders," added Daisy.

"Wearing raincoats and sunglasses?" asked Great-aunt Iris.

"Yes!" cried Jack and Daisy.

"Spies," muttered Great-aunt Iris. She thought fast.

"Jack – spread the rug and lay out cups and saucers.

"Daisy – make a pot of tea, cut
a lemon into slices and put out the
biscuits." There was a determined
look on her long, bony face. "We'll
beat them yet!"

Great-aunt Iris carefully lifted the
shrinking violet out of her pocket.

She ripped one of the tiny flowers into pieces and sprinkled them into the teapot.

There was a rattle of falling rock and the sound of gruff voices.

"Quick!" cried Great-aunt Iris. "Hide behind that bush!"

Jack pointed to the rope hanging over the edge of the volcano. "What about *that*?" he whispered.

Great-aunt Iris's eyes twinkled. "They'll think we're down the volcano," she said gleefully.

8. Disgraceful Manners

The three spies were hot and
thirsty when they reached the
top.

Daisy shivered. They looked
meaner than ever close up.

"Look, they've made tea," said
the first spy, staring at the tartan

rug and the cups and saucers all laid out nicely.

His friend pointed to the rope. "They must still be in the volcano."

The third man smirked. "Then they won't want any tea . . ." He cut the rope. "Ever again."

The three spies fell about laughing nastily.

"Disgraceful manners," muttered Great-aunt Iris from behind the bush.

"I'll be mother," said the first spy. He grabbed the pot and slopped out the tea. "Milk or lemon?"

"Both," said the second.

The third only nodded because he was stuffing his face with all the chocolate biscuits.

The three spies slurped their tea in one gulp and wiped the crumbs from their mouths with their sleeves.

Ugh! thought Jack and Daisy.

Then the most extraordinary thing happened – the three spies shrank to the size of beetles!

"Help! Save us!" squeaked the tiny spies as they scurried about on the rug and tripped over the teaspoons.

"We'll save you, all right," said Great-aunt Iris in a stern voice. She leapt up and scooped them all into her specimen box.

"What are you going to do with them?" asked Jack.

Great-aunt Iris snapped the lid of the box shut.

"Dr Grey-Matter can decide that," she replied. "The important thing is that the shrinking violet is safe."

She beamed at Jack and Daisy. "Now it's about time we set off back home."

9. Such an Adventure!

G reat-aunt Iris, Jack and Daisy
sat around the tea table in the
pink and white cottage.

"So, Jack," said Great-aunt Iris,
sweetly. "Now you know that not
all plants come from seed packets."

"And not all Great-aunts spend

their time pruning roses, picking caterpillars off cabbages and weeding carrots," said Daisy.

"And some things," said Great-aunt Iris with a smile, "are best kept secret from some people."

At that moment, Mr and Mrs Primly-Proper knocked on the door and walked into the room.

"Gracious!" cried Mrs Primly-Proper, looking quite pink in the face. "We've had such an adventure!"

"We certainly did!" agreed Mr Primly-Proper. "We had a puncture on our way over and then for a moment we thought we might have got lost in the maze!"

"Well, not really *lost*," said Mrs

Primly-Proper hurriedly. "Just taken
a wrong turning, perhaps."

"Dear me!" replied Great-aunt
Iris. "That *is* an adventure. Sit
down and tell us all about it."

She winked at Jack and Daisy. "We've had such a quiet week, haven't we, dears?"

"We've never had a week quite like it," replied Daisy, politely.

Jack grinned but didn't say anything. His finger was stuck in the teacup handle again!